Little Look and Find®

MARVEL
SPIDER-MAN

P9-CCO-452

pi kids® Phoenix International Publications, Inc.

Chicago • London • New York • Hamburg • Mexico City • Paris • Sydney

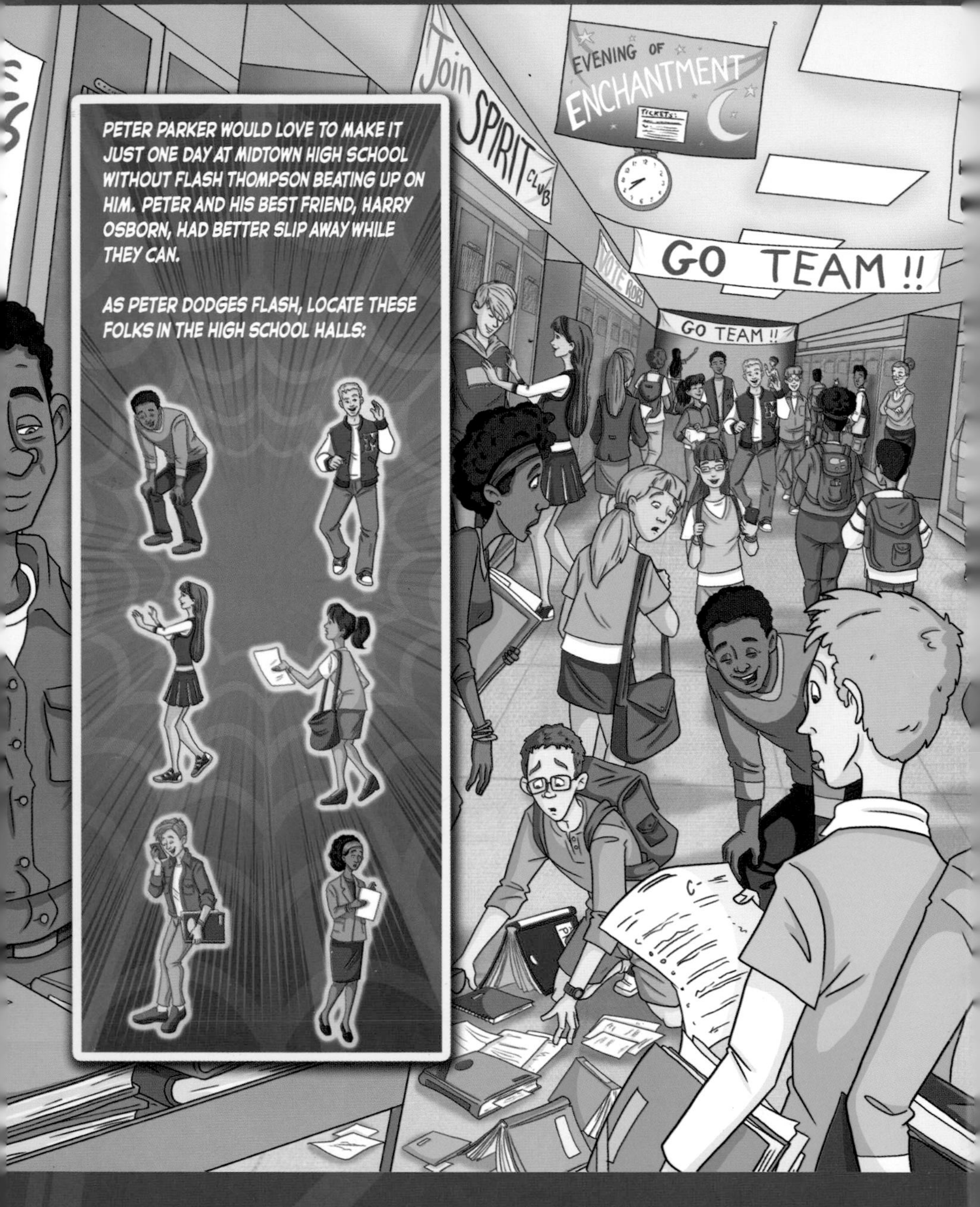
PETER PARKER WOULD LOVE TO MAKE IT JUST ONE DAY AT MIDTOWN HIGH SCHOOL WITHOUT FLASH THOMPSON BEATING UP ON HIM. PETER AND HIS BEST FRIEND, HARRY OSBORN, HAD BETTER SLIP AWAY WHILE THEY CAN.
AS PETER DODGES FLASH, LOCATE THESE FOLKS IN THE HIGH SCHOOL HALLS:
Join SPIRIT CLUB
EVENING OF ENCHANTMENT
TICKETS:
GO TEAM !!
VOTE ROBI
GO TEAM !!
C-

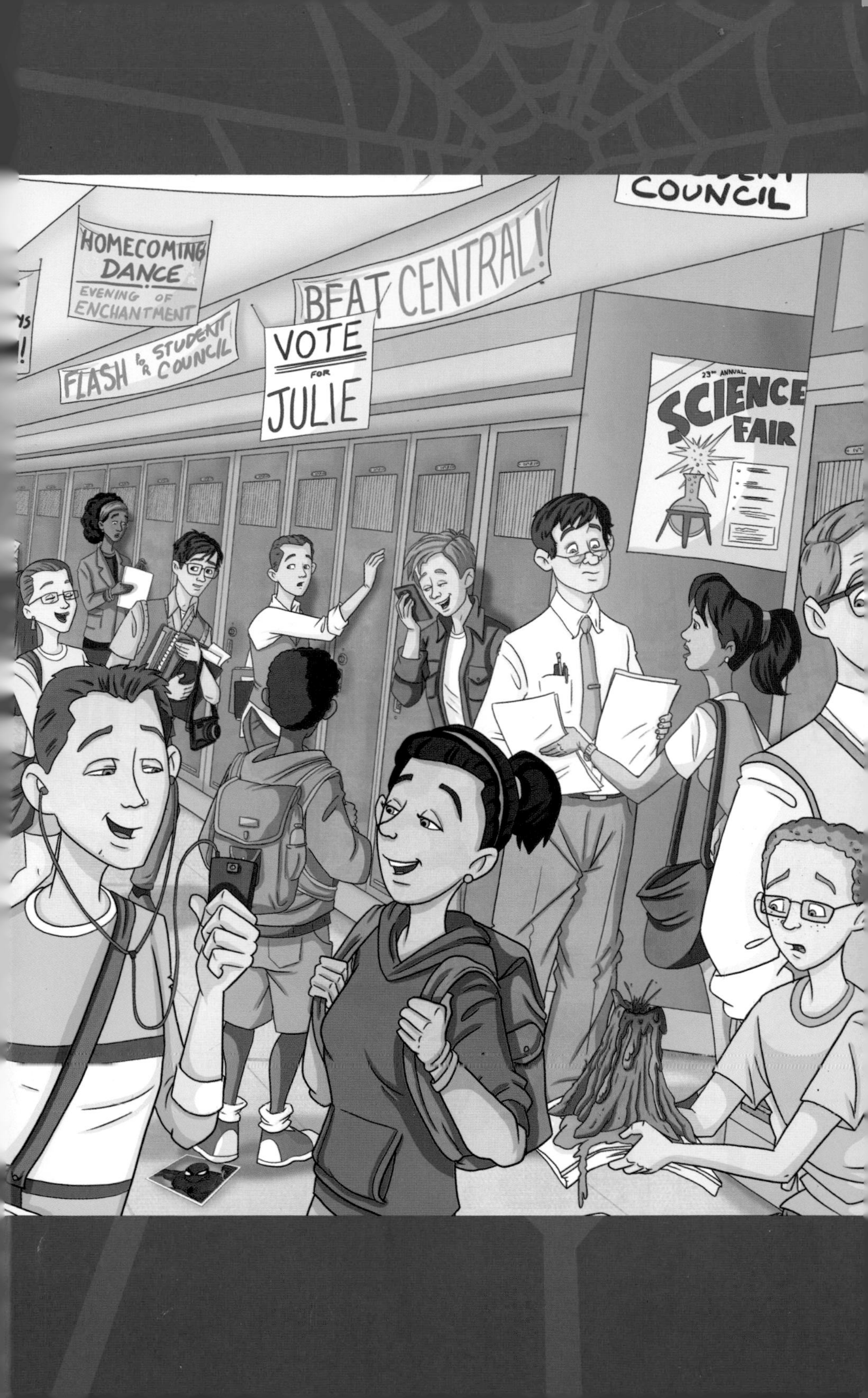
COUNCIL
HOMECOMING DANCE
EVENING OF ENCHANTMENT
BEAT CENTRAL!
FLASH FOR STUDENT COUNCIL
VOTE FOR JULIE
23RD ANNUAL
SCIENCE FAIR

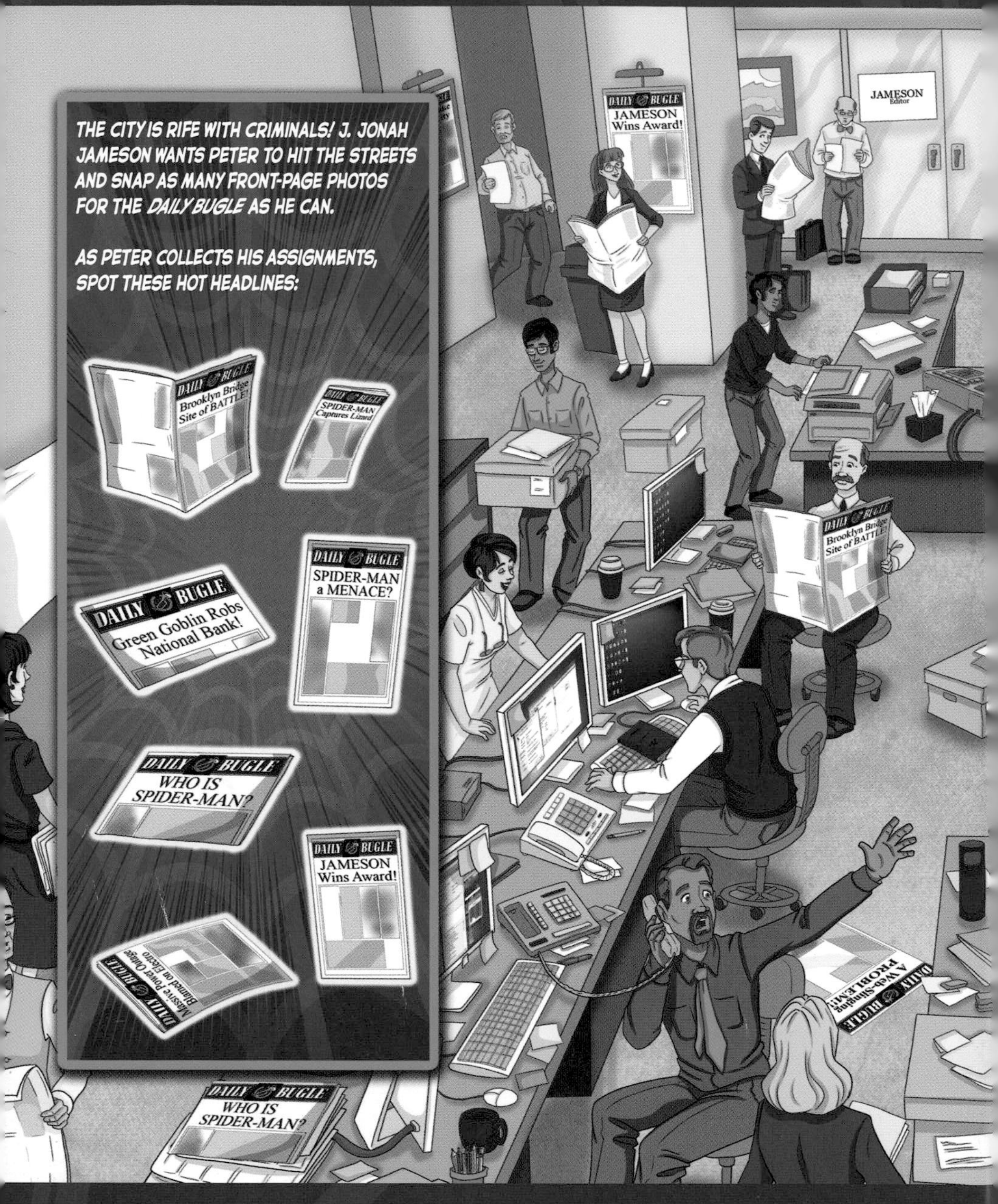
THE CITY IS RIFE WITH CRIMINALS! J. JONAH JAMESON WANTS PETER TO HIT THE STREETS AND SNAP AS MANY FRONT-PAGE PHOTOS FOR THE *DAILY BUGLE* AS HE CAN.
AS PETER COLLECTS HIS ASSIGNMENTS, SPOT THESE HOT HEADLINES:
DAILY BUGLE Brooklyn Bridge Site of BATTLE!
DAILY BUGLE SPIDER-MAN Captures Lizard
DAILY BUGLE SPIDER-MAN a MENACE?
DAILY BUGLE Green Goblin Robs National Bank!
DAILY BUGLE WHO IS SPIDER-MAN?
DAILY BUGLE JAMESON Wins Award!
DAILY BUGLE Massive Power Outage Blamed on Electro
JAMESON Editor
DAILY BUGLE JAMESON Wins Award!
DAILY BUGLE Brooklyn Bridge Site of BATTLE!
DAILY BUGLE A Web-Slinging PROBLEM!
DAILY BUGLE WHO IS SPIDER-MAN?

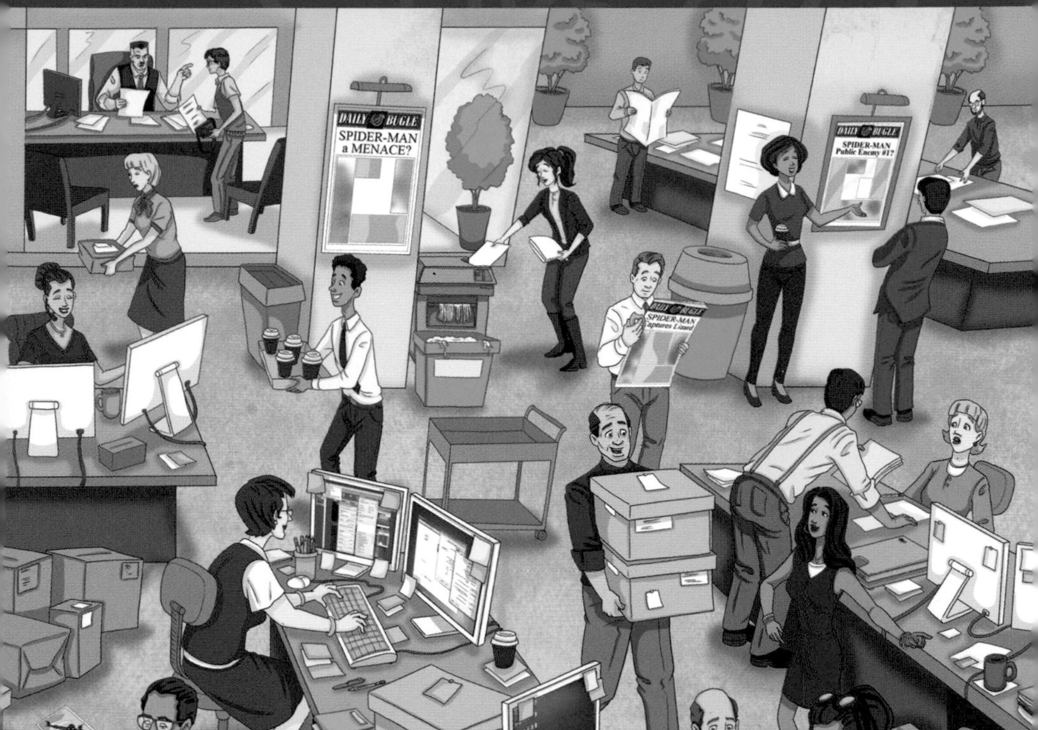
DAILY BUGLE
SPIDER-MAN a MENACE?
DAILY BUGLE
SPIDER-MAN Public Enemy #1?
DAILY BUGLE
SPIDER-MAN Captures Lizard
DAILY BUGLE
Sandman on the Loose!
DAILY BUGLE
Massive Power Outage Blamed on Electro
DAILY BUGLE
Green Goblin Robs National Bank!

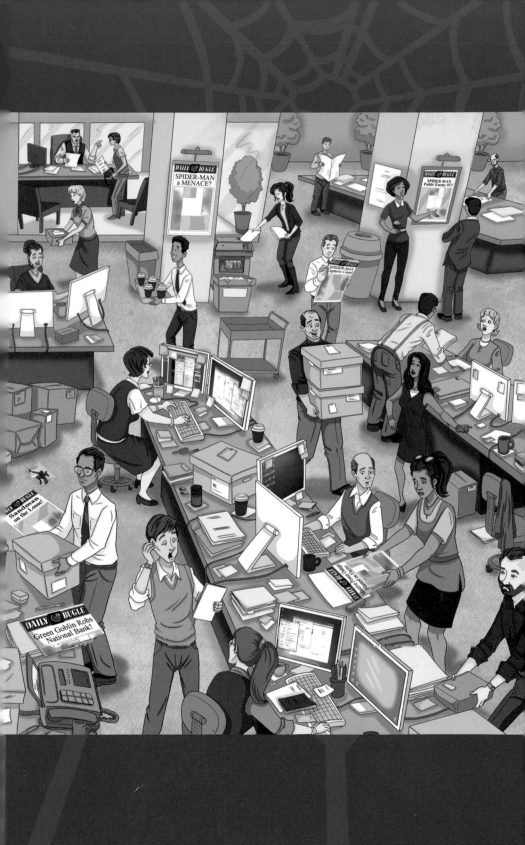

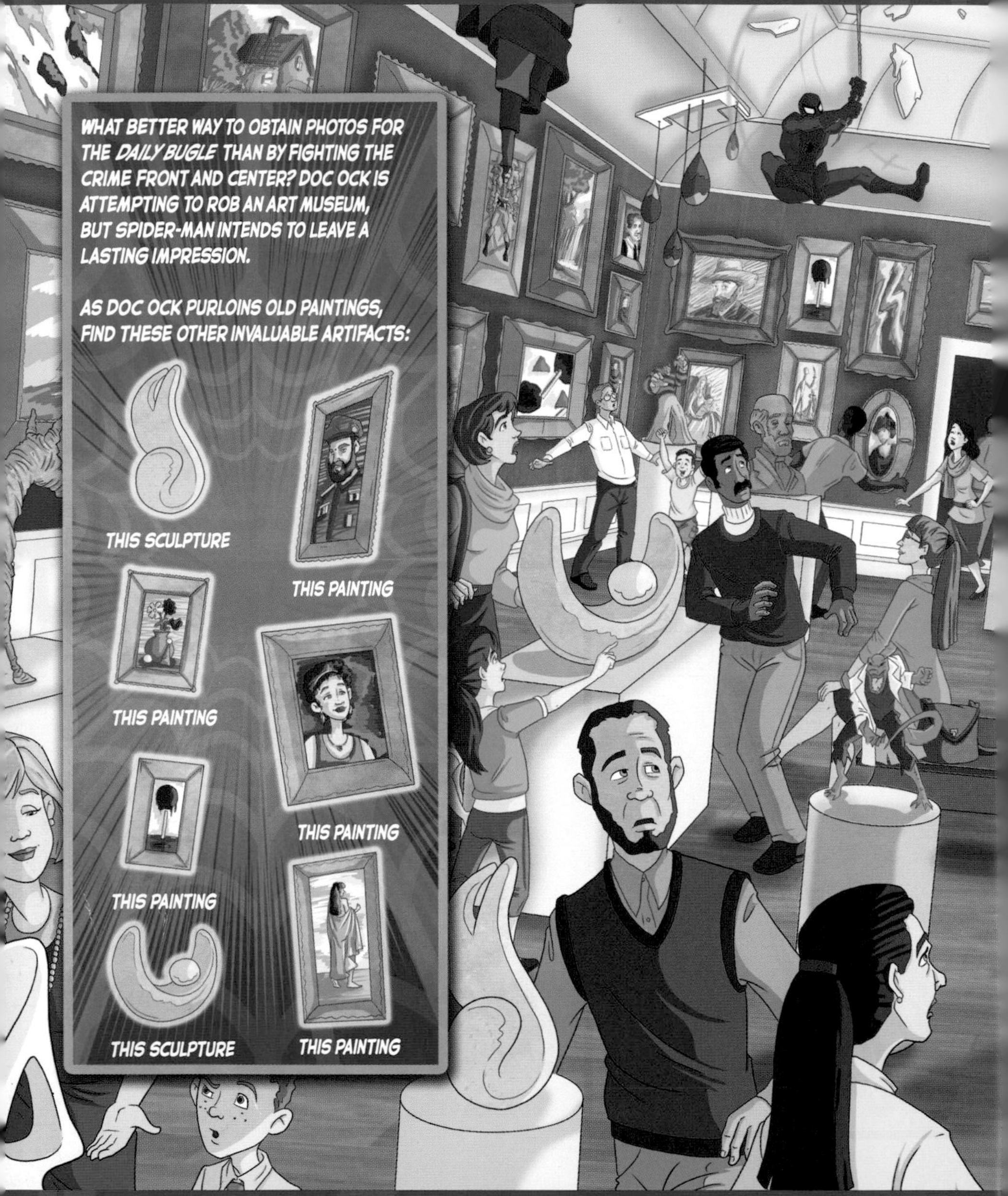
WHAT BETTER WAY TO OBTAIN PHOTOS FOR THE *DAILY BUGLE* THAN BY FIGHTING THE CRIME FRONT AND CENTER? DOC OCK IS ATTEMPTING TO ROB AN ART MUSEUM, BUT SPIDER-MAN INTENDS TO LEAVE A LASTING IMPRESSION.
AS DOC OCK PURLOINS OLD PAINTINGS, FIND THESE OTHER INVALUABLE ARTIFACTS:
THIS SCULPTURE
THIS PAINTING
THIS PAINTING
THIS PAINTING
THIS PAINTING
THIS SCULPTURE
THIS PAINTING

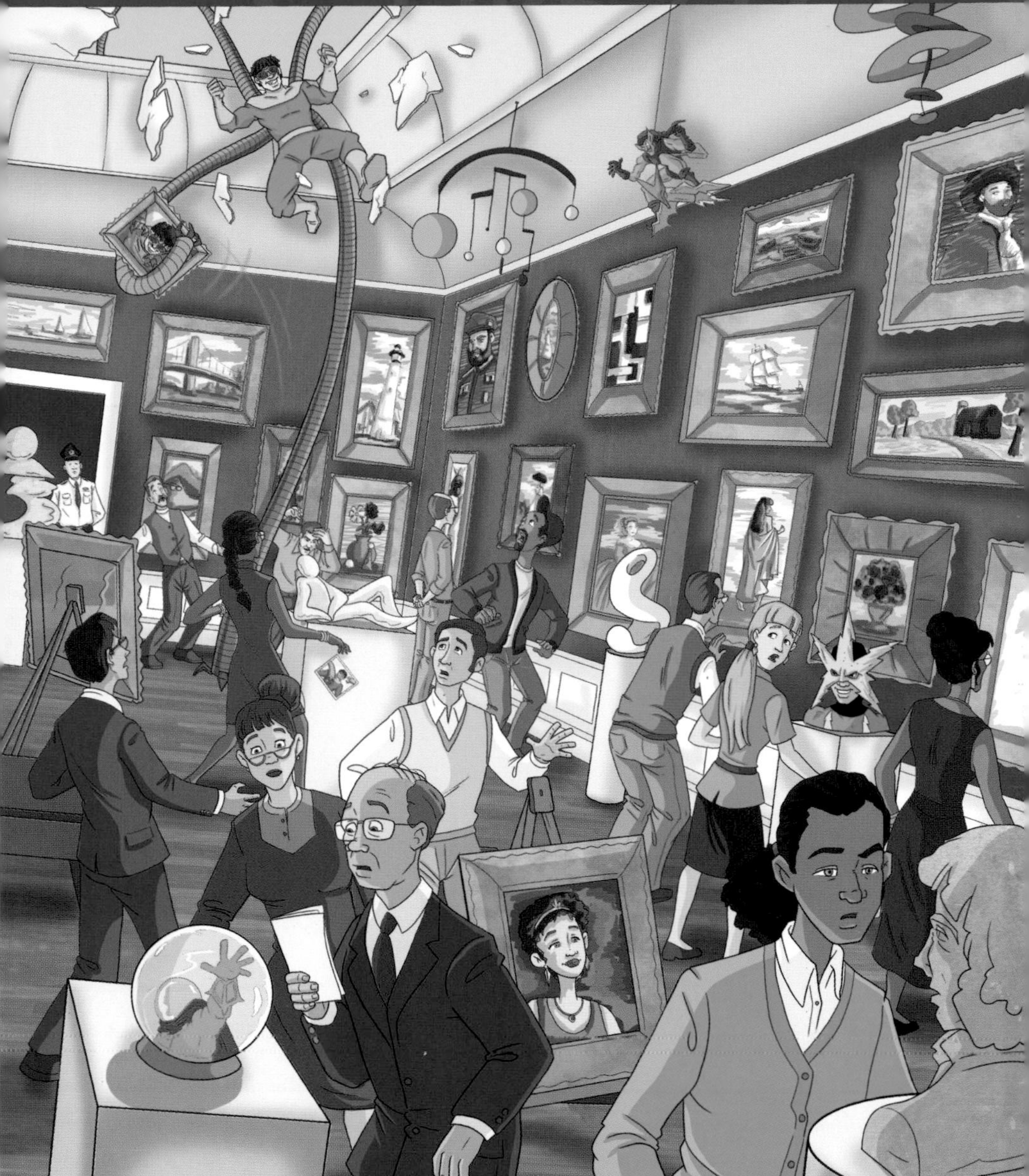

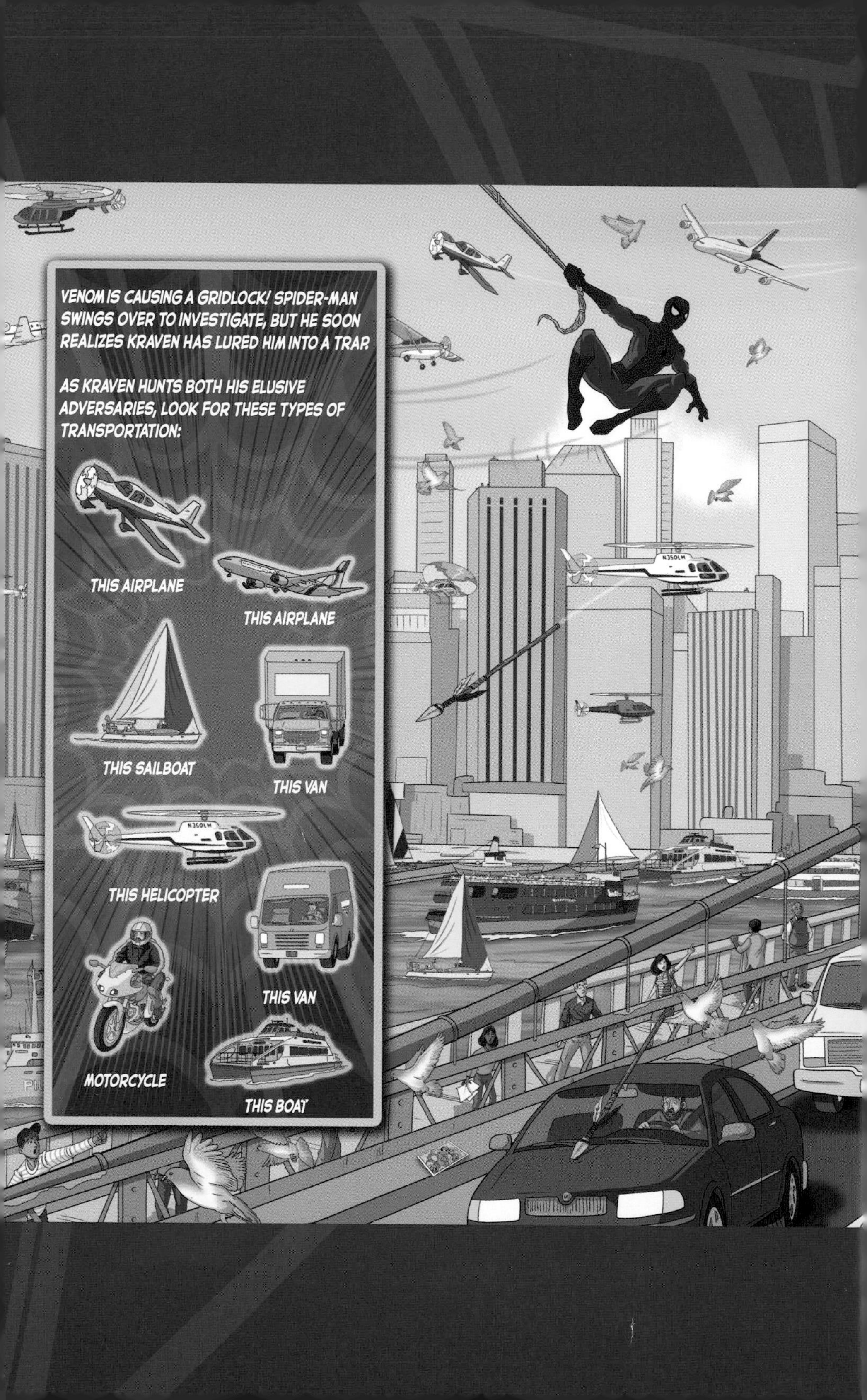
VENOM IS CAUSING A GRIDLOCK! SPIDER-MAN SWINGS OVER TO INVESTIGATE, BUT HE SOON REALIZES KRAVEN HAS LURED HIM INTO A TRAP.
AS KRAVEN HUNTS BOTH HIS ELUSIVE ADVERSARIES, LOOK FOR THESE TYPES OF TRANSPORTATION:
THIS AIRPLANE
THIS AIRPLANE
THIS SAILBOAT
THIS VAN
THIS HELICOPTER
THIS VAN
MOTORCYCLE
THIS BOAT

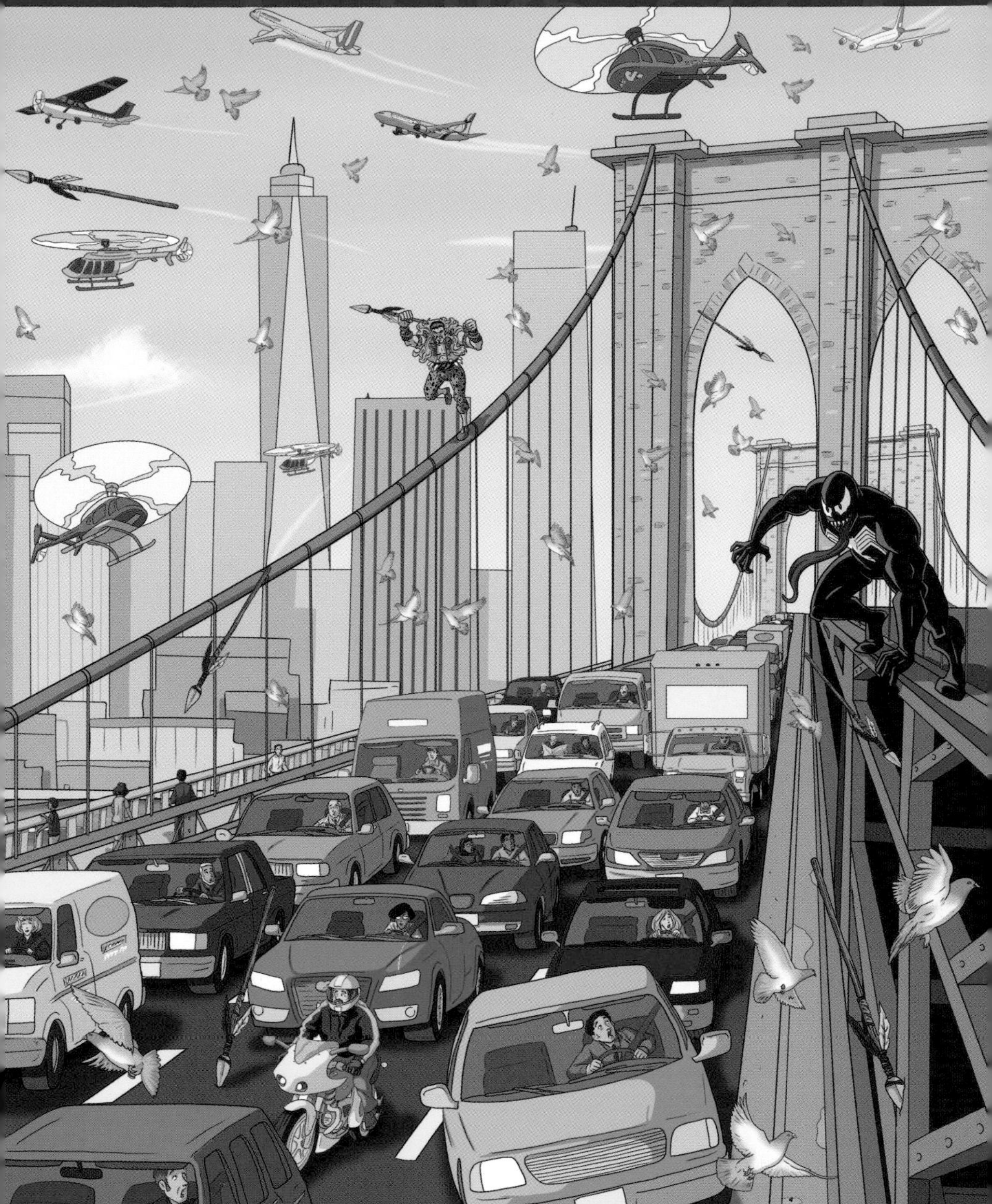

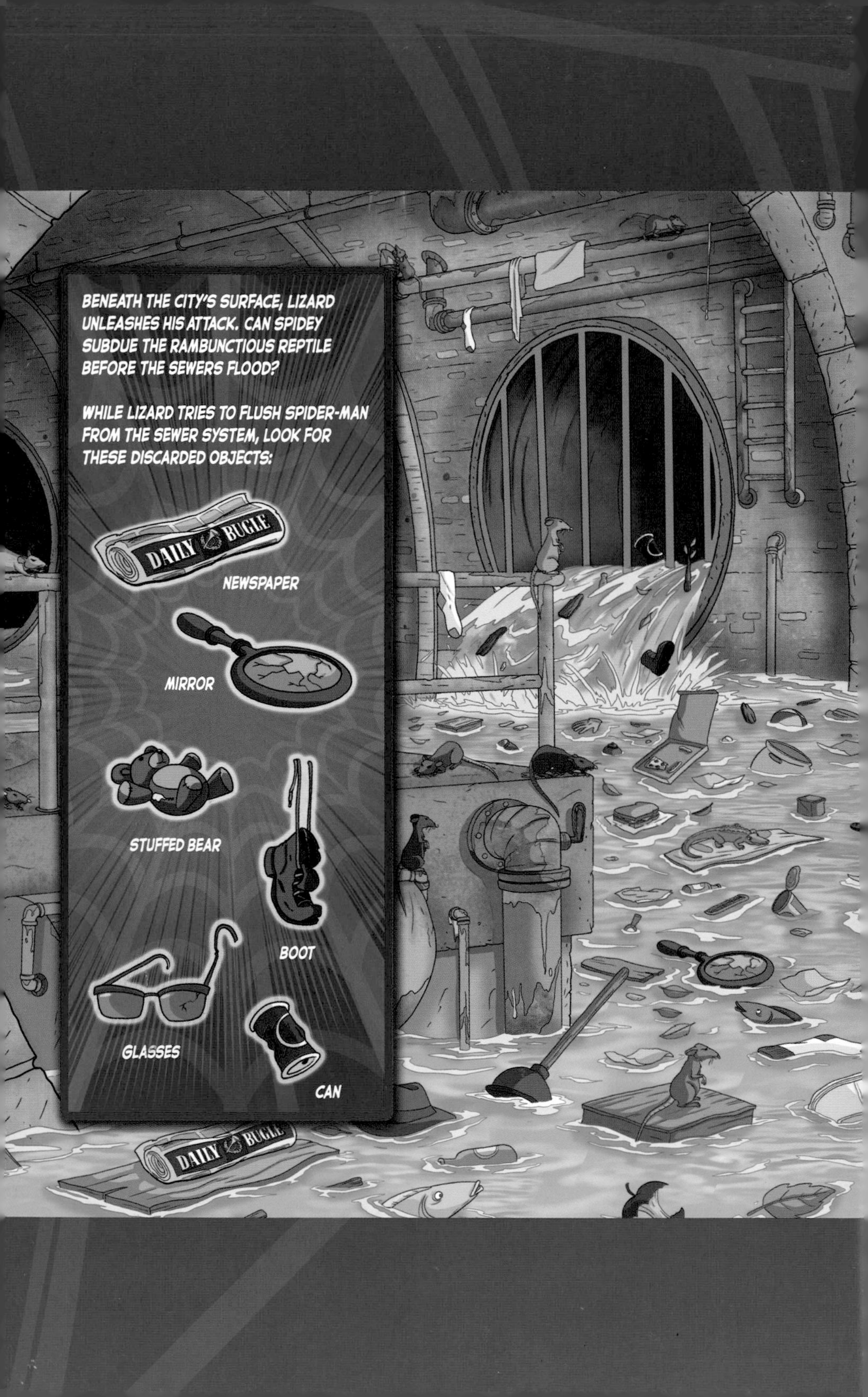
BENEATH THE CITY'S SURFACE, LIZARD UNLEASHES HIS ATTACK. CAN SPIDEY SUBDUE THE RAMBUNCTIOUS REPTILE BEFORE THE SEWERS FLOOD?
WHILE LIZARD TRIES TO FLUSH SPIDER-MAN FROM THE SEWER SYSTEM, LOOK FOR THESE DISCARDED OBJECTS:
DAILY BUGLE
NEWSPAPER
MIRROR
STUFFED BEAR
BOOT
GLASSES
CAN
DAILY BUGLE

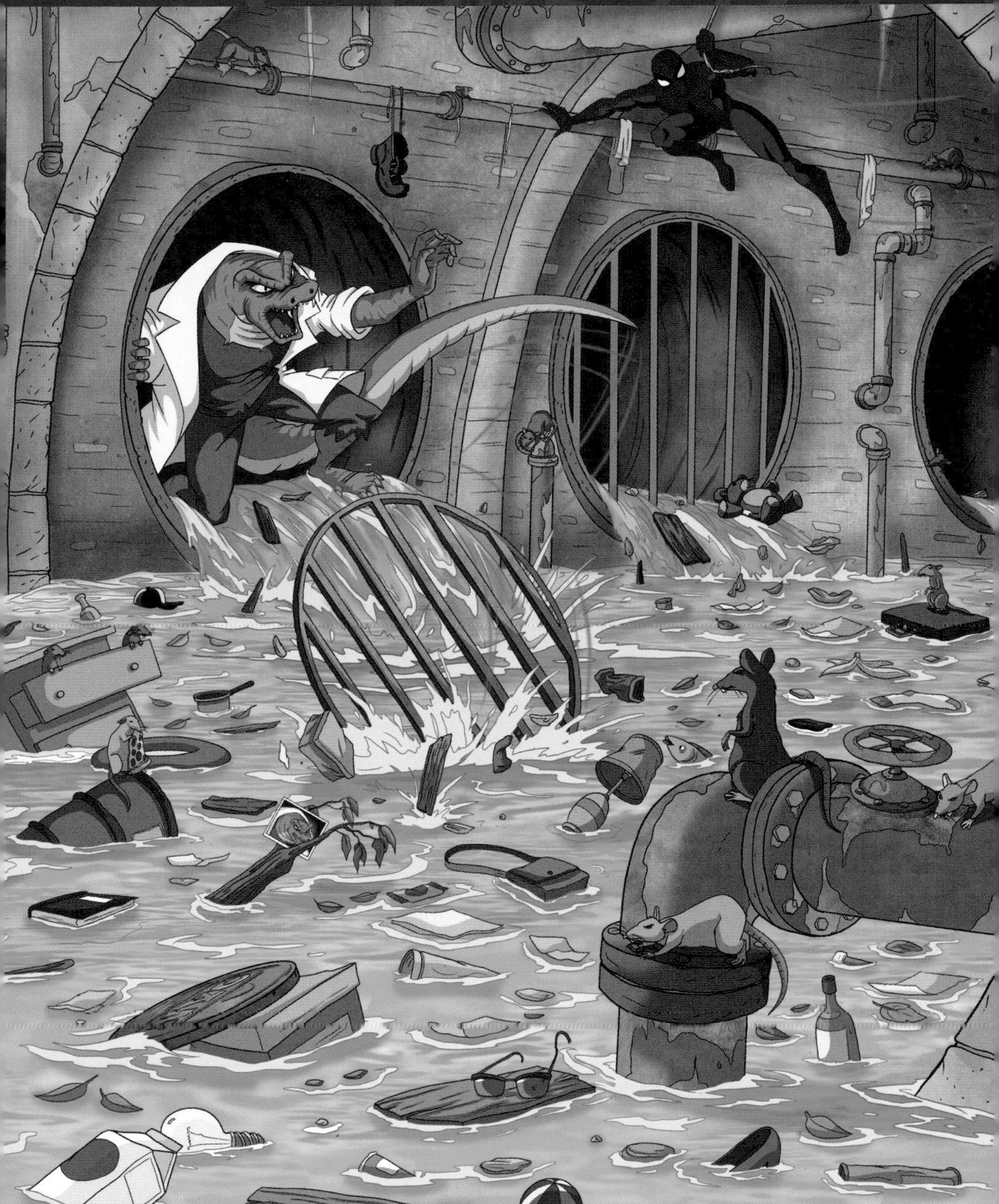

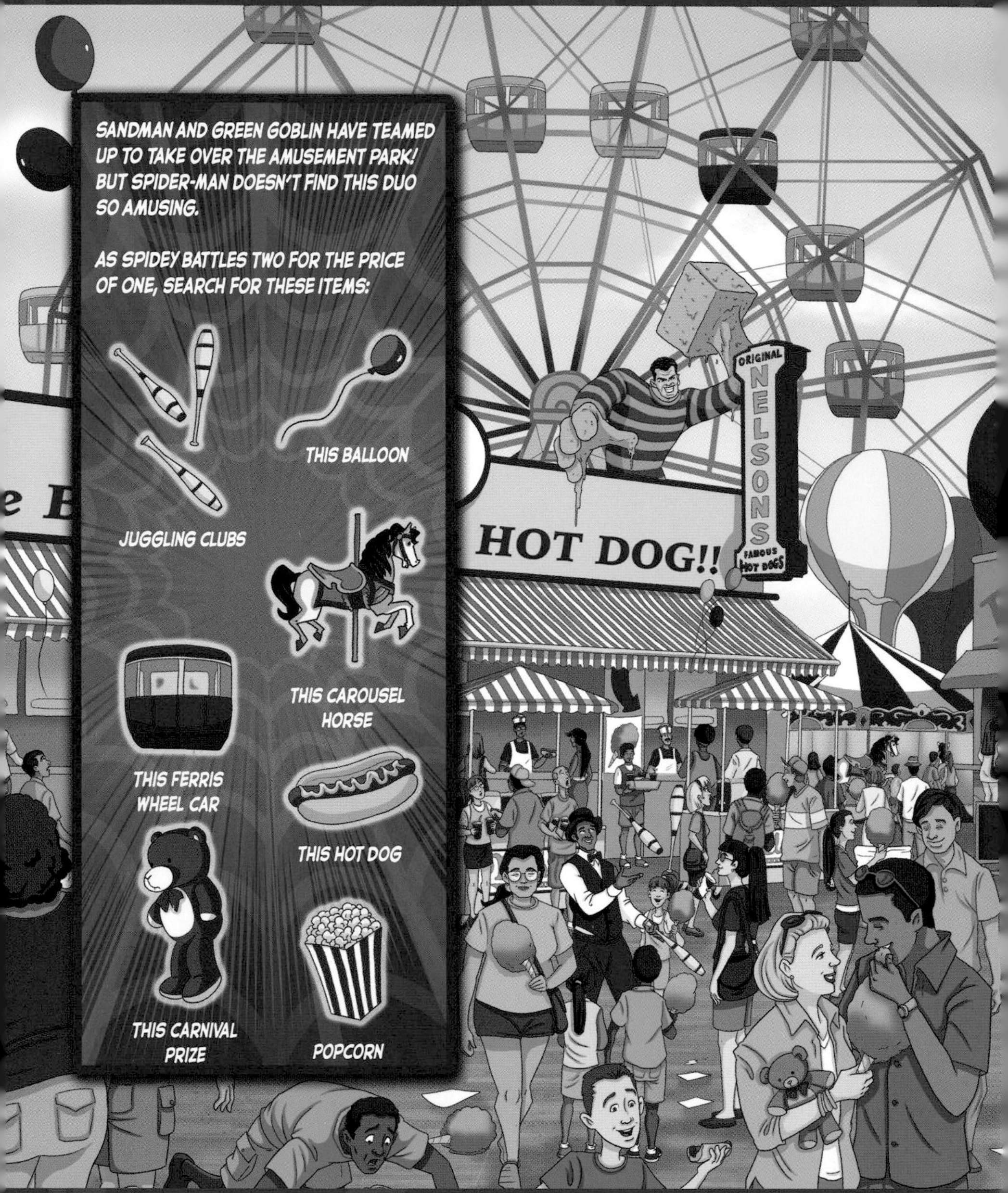
SANDMAN AND GREEN GOBLIN HAVE TEAMED UP TO TAKE OVER THE AMUSEMENT PARK! BUT SPIDER-MAN DOESN'T FIND THIS DUO SO AMUSING.
AS SPIDEY BATTLES TWO FOR THE PRICE OF ONE, SEARCH FOR THESE ITEMS:
JUGGLING CLUBS
THIS BALLOON
THIS CAROUSEL HORSE
THIS FERRIS WHEEL CAR
THIS HOT DOG
THIS CARNIVAL PRIZE
POPCORN
ORIGINAL
NELSONS
FAMOUS HOT DOGS
HOT DOG!!

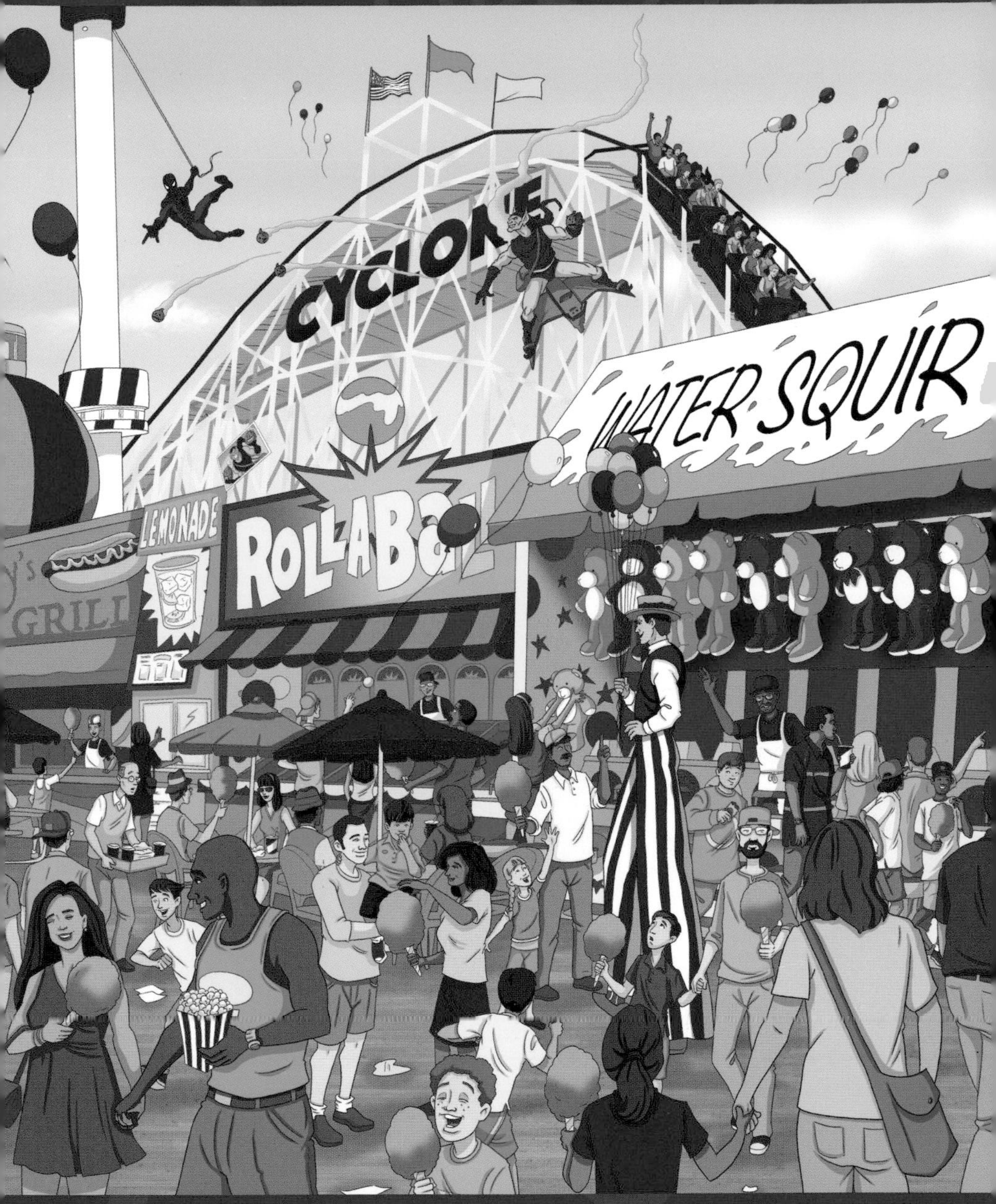
CYCLONE
WATER SQUIR
LEMONADE
ROLLABALL
GRILL

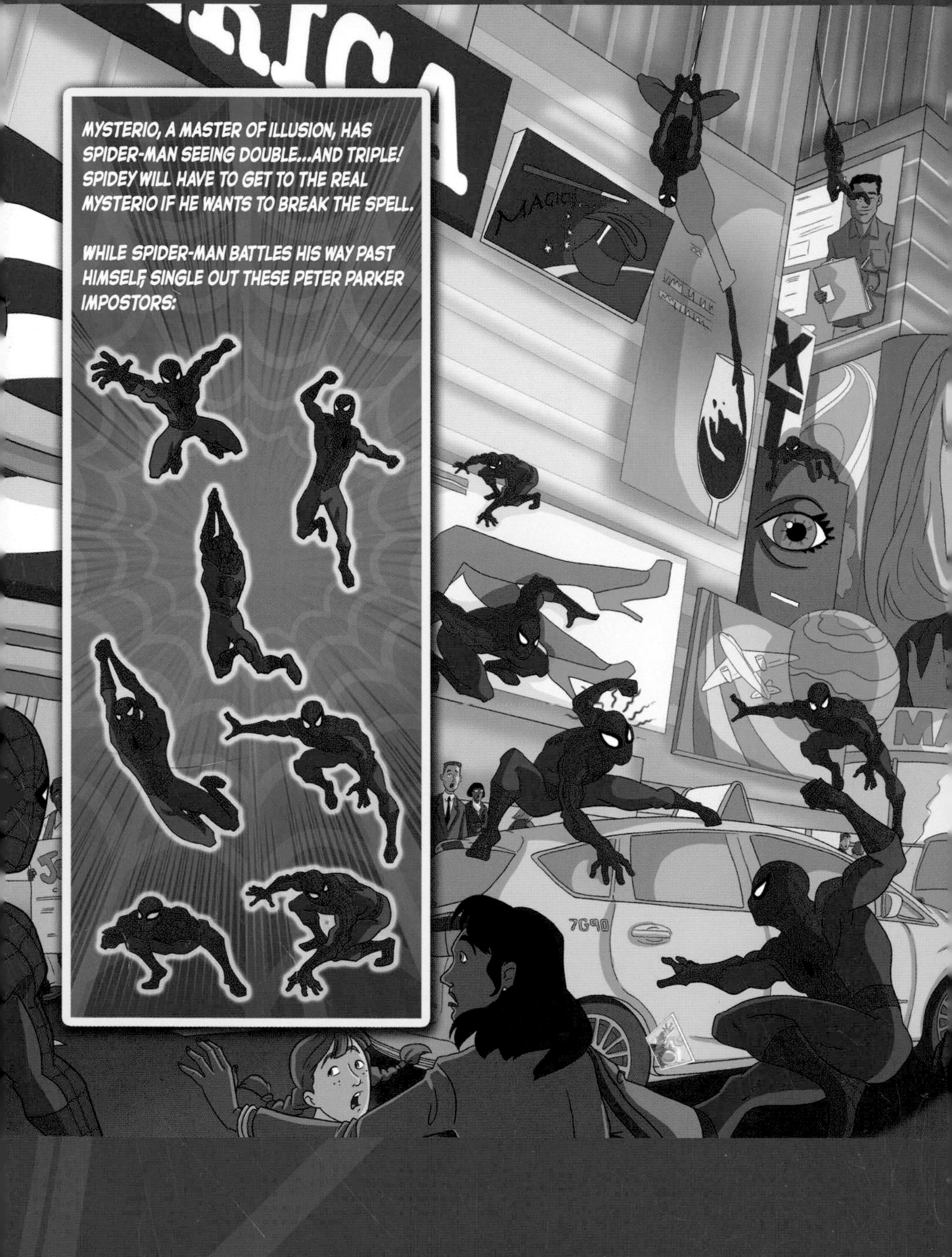
MYSTERIO, A MASTER OF ILLUSION, HAS SPIDER-MAN SEEING DOUBLE...AND TRIPLE! SPIDEY WILL HAVE TO GET TO THE REAL MYSTERIO IF HE WANTS TO BREAK THE SPELL.
WHILE SPIDER-MAN BATTLES HIS WAY PAST HIMSELF, SINGLE OUT THESE PETER PARKER IMPOSTORS:
7G90

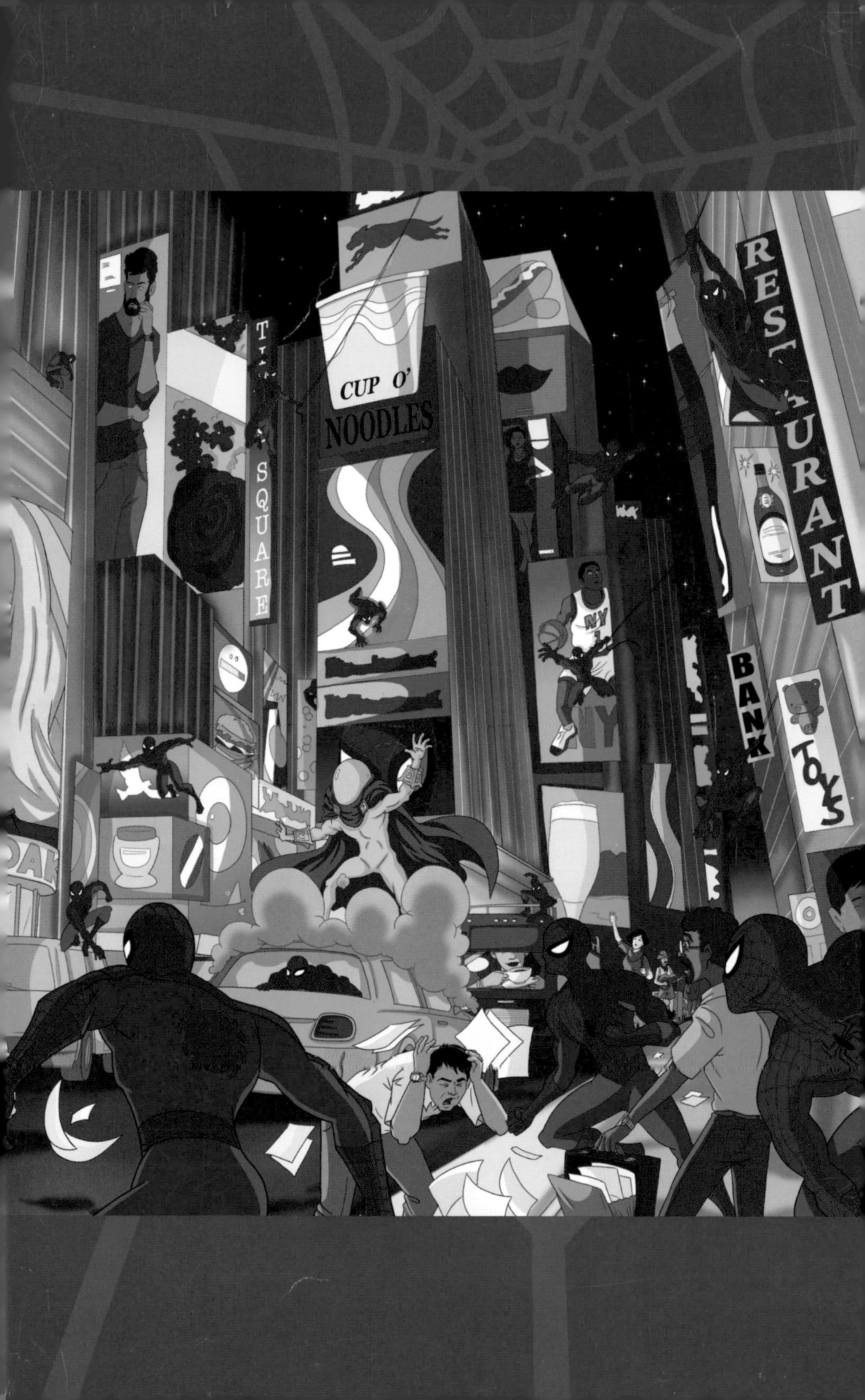
CUP O'
NOODLES
SQUARE
BANK
TOYS
NY

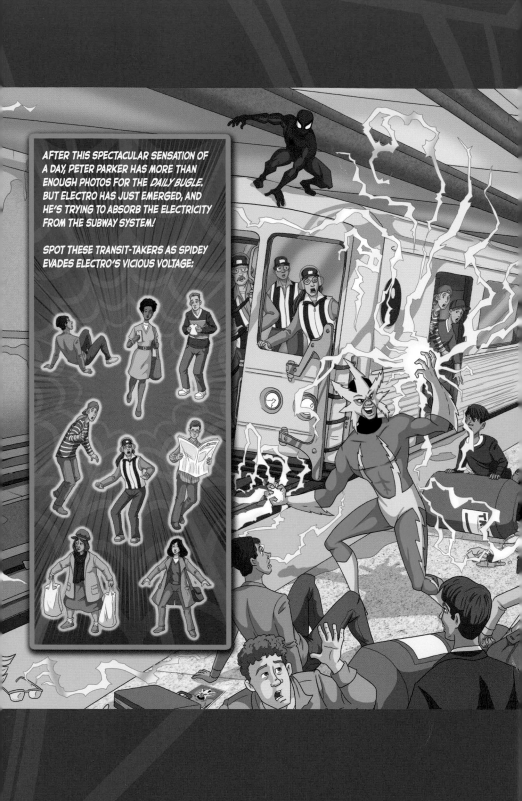

AFTER THIS SPECTACULAR SENSATION OF A DAY, PETER PARKER HAS MORE THAN ENOUGH PHOTOS FOR THE *DAILY BUGLE*. BUT ELECTRO HAS JUST EMERGED, AND HE'S TRYING TO ABSORB THE ELECTRICITY FROM THE SUBWAY SYSTEM!

SPOT THESE TRANSIT-TAKERS AS SPIDEY EVADES ELECTRO'S VICIOUS VOLTAGE:

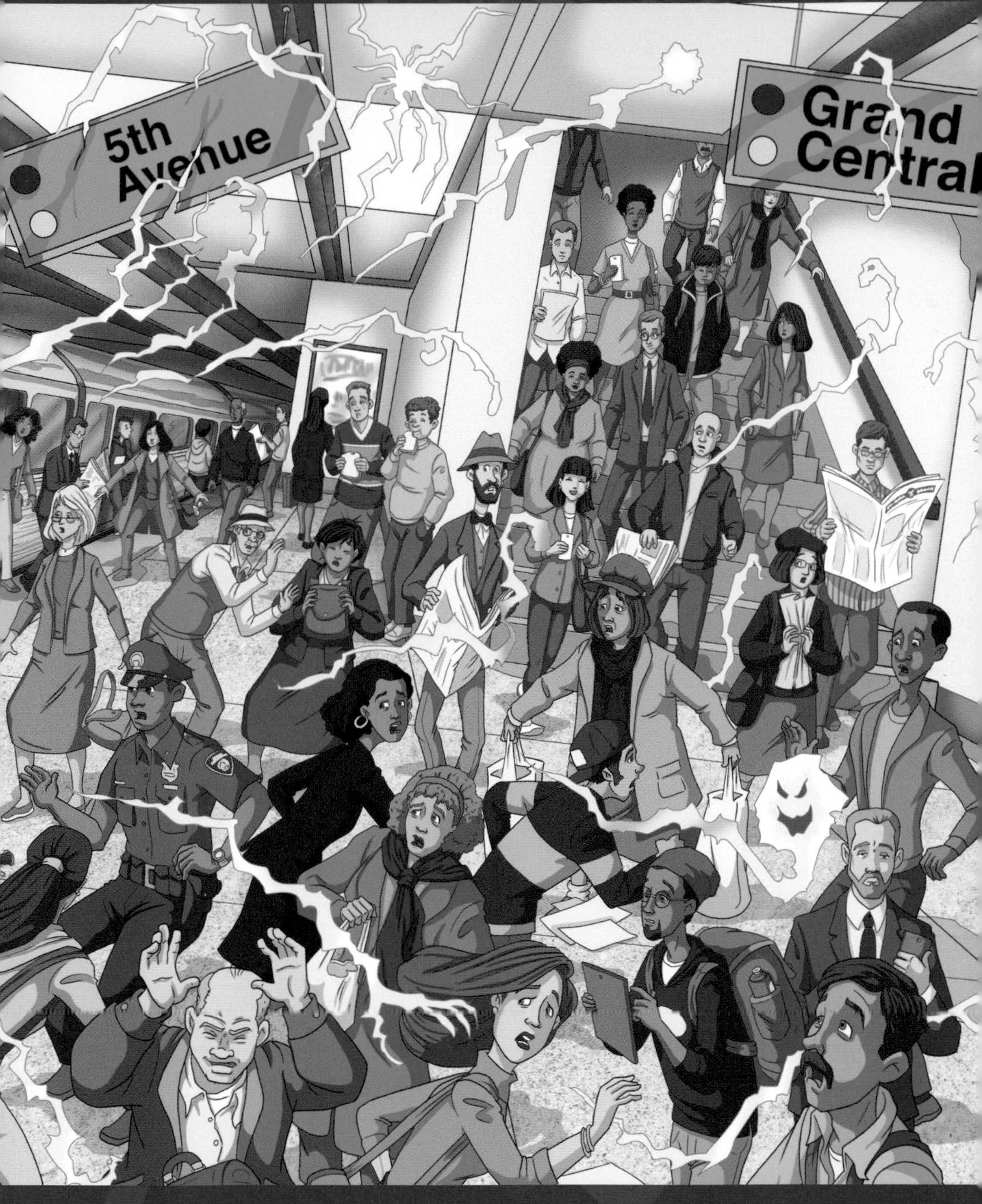
5th Avenue
Grand Central

HURRY BACK TO SCHOOL BEFORE THE TARDY BELL RINGS AND FIND THESE ITEMS SCATTERED IN THE HALL:

PHYSICS
THIS TEXTBOOK
SCIENCE PROJECT
SCIENCE FAIR
THIS BOOK BAG
THIS POSTER
EVENING OF ENCHANTMENT
BEAT CENTRAL!
THIS BANNER
THIS BANNER

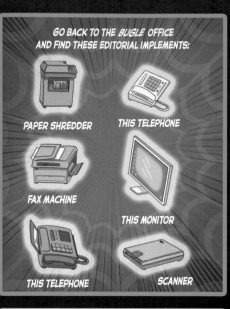

GO BACK TO THE *BUGLE* OFFICE AND FIND THESE EDITORIAL IMPLEMENTS:

PAPER SHREDDER
THIS TELEPHONE
FAX MACHINE
THIS MONITOR
THIS TELEPHONE
SCANNER

TAKE ANOTHER TOUR THROUGH THE ART MUSEUM AND POINT OUT THESE VILLAINOUS VISAGES:

MYSTERIO
ELECTRO
LIZARD
DOC OCK
SANDMAN
KRAVEN
GREEN GOBLIN

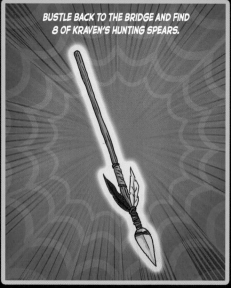

BUSTLE BACK TO THE BRIDGE AND FIND 8 OF KRAVEN'S HUNTING SPEARS.

TRUDGE BACK THROUGH THE SEWER SLUDGE TO FIND THESE INDUSTRIAL ITEMS:

LADDER

THIS PIPE

MANHOLE COVER

VALVE

THIS PIPE

GRATE

PASS THE TIME IN LINE AT THE AMUSEMENT PARK BY FINDING 20 TUFTS OF COTTON CANDY.

REVISIT MYSTERIO'S MIND-BENDING ILLUSION AND SPOT THESE ALLURING ADVERTISEMENTS:

CUP O' NOODLES

CAUTION: ELECTRO'S HIGH VOLTAGE IS HAZARDOUS TO YOUR HEALTH! SCURRY BACK TO THE SUBWAY TO SPOT—AND STEER CLEAR OF—THESE ERRATIC BOLTS OF ELECTRICITY:

IN A HURRY TO VANQUISH VILLAINS AROUND EVERY CORNER, SPIDER-MAN MANAGED TO DROP SOME OF HIS BEST SNAPSHOTS FOR THE *DAILY BUGLE.* GO BACK AND FIND ONE DROPPED PHOTOGRAPH IN EACH LOCATION—J. JONAH JAMESON WON'T TAKE NO FOR AN ANSWER.

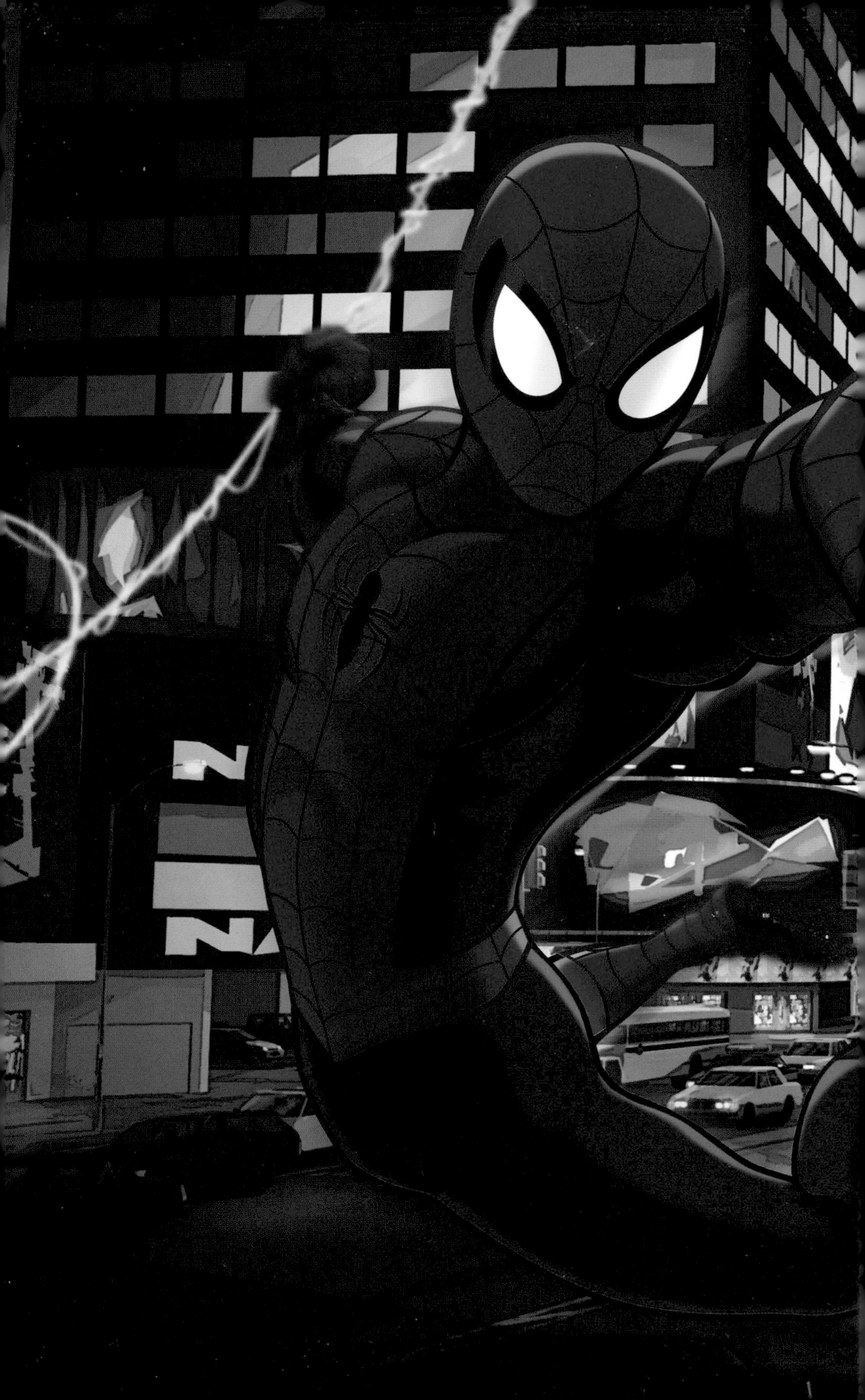